Valerie Thomas and Korky Paul

Winnie's Magic Moments

Winnie's Magic Wand

Winnie's New Computer

Winnie at the Seaside

OXFORD
UNIVERSITY PRESS

OXFORD
UNIVERSITY PRESS

Great Clarendon Street, Oxford OX2 6DP
Oxford University Press is a department of the University of Oxford.
It furthers the University's objective of excellence in research, scholarship,
and education by publishing worldwide in
Oxford   New York

Auckland   Cape Town   Dar es Salaam   Hong Kong   Karachi
Kuala Lumpur   Madrid   Melbourne   Mexico City   Nairobi
New Delhi   Shanghai   Taipei   Toronto

With offices in

Argentina   Austria   Brazil   Chile   Czech Republic   France   Greece
Guatemala   Hungary   Italy   Japan Poland   Portugal   Singapore
South Korea   Switzerland   Thailand   Turkey   Ukraine   Vietnam

Oxford is a registered trade mark of Oxford University Press
in the UK and in certain other countries

This book first published 2009

Winnie's Magic Wand first published 2002
Winnie's New Computer first published 2003
Winnie at the Seaside first published 2005

The stories are complete and unabridged

6 8 10 9 7 5

British Library Cataloguing in Publication Data
Data available

ISBN: 978-0-19-272907-1

Printed in Singapore

Paper used in the production of this book is a natural,
recyclable product made from wood grown in sustainable forests.
The manufacturing process conforms to the environmental
regulations of the country of origin

www.korkypaul.com

Winnie's
Magic Wand

Winnie the Witch jumped out of bed.
It was a special day. It was the day of the
Witches' Magic Show, and Winnie was
making a wonderful new spell.

She felt nervous.
'I hope nothing goes wrong,' she said.
Wilbur felt nervous too. I expect something
will go wrong, he thought.

'What shall I wear?' said Winnie.
She got out her party dress.
Oh no! She had spilt red jelly on it!

Winnie threw the dress into the washing machine.
Then she threw in her towels, her pyjamas,
and her stripy tights.

She turned on the washing machine.
Swish, swish, clunk, it went.

When the washing machine had finished
going swish, swish, clunk, Winnie took out
the clothes and hung them on the line.

But her magic wand had been washed as well. Oh no!

'I hope it still works,' Winnie said.

Winnie dried the wand with a towel.

'I'll try it out,' she said. 'Something easy. I'll change this apple into an orange.'

She closed her eyes, waved her wand, and shouted,

ABRACADABRA!

Suddenly there was an apple tree growing in her kitchen.
'Bother!' said Winnie. 'That wand's not working properly.'

Winnie dried the wand with her hair-drier.

'That's better,' she said. 'I'll try again.
I'll turn this apple tree back into an apple again.'
She picked up the wand, and shouted,

ABRACADABRA!

This time, the apple tree turned into an enormous apple pie.

'Oh no! **Oh no!**' Winnie moaned.
Now she really was worried.
It was nearly time for the Magic Show.
The wonderful new spell would be a disaster.

Wilbur was worried too.

Then Wilbur had an idea.
He ran out of the house,

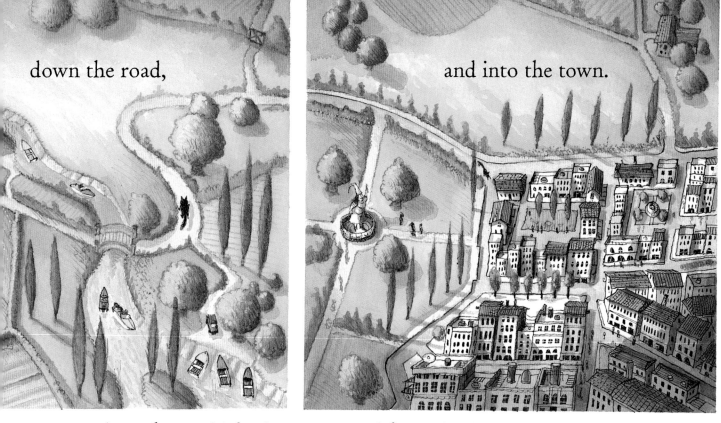

down the road,

and into the town.

Perhaps *he* could find a new wand for Winnie.
He looked in all the shops.

But no magic wands.

Then, around the corner, he saw a little shop.
In the window was a big box of wands!

Wilbur grabbed one and galloped off home.

It was getting late.
Soon it would be too late for the Magic
Show. Winnie was very, very worried.

What could she do?

Then Wilbur ran through the cat flap with the new wand.

'Oh Wilbur!' cried Winnie. 'You are a clever cat.'

She didn't even have time to put on her party dress.
She jumped on her broomstick,
Wilbur jumped onto her shoulder,
and off they went.

They arrived just in time for Winnie's spell.
Everyone was sitting there, feeling excited.
Winnie always did something special.

'First,' announced Winnie, 'I will turn my
beautiful black cat into a green cat.'

She waved her wand, and shouted,

ABRACADABRA!

Wilbur waited . . .
        Everyone waited . . .

Winnie tried again.

Nothing.

At last, a bunch of paper flowers
popped out of the end of
the trick wand.

One of the witches started to laugh.
Soon everyone was laughing.
They laughed, they screamed,
they shrieked and fell off their chairs.

'What a clever joke, Winnie,' they cried.
'Where did you get that wand?'
Winnie smiled. But she didn't say anything.

And neither did Wilbur.

Winnie's
New Computer

Winnie the Witch had a new computer. She was very excited. Her cat, Wilbur, was excited too. He thought something interesting might happen and he didn't want to miss it.

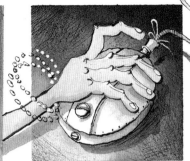

Winnie plugged in the computer,
turned it on, and clicked the mouse.
'Come on, mouse,' she said.

Is that a *mouse*? thought Wilbur.
It doesn't look like one.

CLICK CLICK

Winnie went on to the internet.
Wilbur wanted a closer look at the mouse.
He patted it.

'Don't touch the mouse, Wilbur!' said Winnie.
'I want to order a new wand!'

Wilbur patted the mouse again. Pat, pat.

Winnie was cross.
She put Wilbur outside.
She didn't notice
that it was raining . . .

Wilbur noticed it was raining. He was getting wet.
He watched Winnie through the window.
She was having a good time.

She ordered her new wand, and then
she visited some websites for witches.
They had some very funny jokes.
'Ha, ha, ha,' laughed Winnie.

Wilbur *wasn't* laughing.
The rain was dripping off his whiskers.
'Meeow,' he cried. ' Meeeoooww!'
But Winnie didn't hear him.

That mouse has put a spell on her, thought Wilbur.

CLICK
CLICK

Plop
plop plop
plop plop
plop Plop Plop
plop plop plop
plop Plop
plop
Plop

Plop, plop, plop.
'What's that noise?'
asked Winnie.

It was the rain.
It was coming through the roof.

'Oh no!' said Winnie. 'The rain
will ruin my new computer!
I need the Roof Repair Spell.'

But she couldn't find her book of spells
or her magic wand anywhere.

'Oh, where are they?' she cried
as the rain plopped down.

At last she found them.
She waved her wand seven
times at the roof, and shouted,

ABRACADABRA!

The roof stopped leaking.
'Thank goodness,' Winnie said.

Then she had a wonderful idea.

'If I scan all my spells into the computer,' she said,
'I won't need my book of spells any more.
I won't need to wave my magic wand.
I'll just use the computer. One click will do the trick.'

So Winnie loaded all her spells into the new computer.
'I'd better try it out,' she said. 'What shall I do?'

'I know, I'll turn Wilbur into a blue cat.'

She let Wilbur inside. She went to the computer, clicked the mouse, and Wilbur was bright blue.

'Good!' said Winnie.
'It works!'

CLICK

CLICK

She clicked the mouse, and Wilbur was a black cat again.
An angry, wet, black cat.

'Well, Wilbur,' said Winnie, 'I won't need my book of spells or my magic wand any more.'

And she put them out for the dustman to take away.

That night, Wilbur waited until
he could hear Winnie snoring.
Then he crept downstairs.

He was going to see about that mouse.

He patted it.
Nothing happened.
'Meeow, grrrrsssss!' he snarled.
He grabbed the mouse, tossed it
into the air, and rolled onto his back.

Winnie had a lovely sleep.
In the morning she came downstairs
for her breakfast.

'Breakfast, Wilbur,' she called.
'Where are you, Wilbur?'

She looked in the garden, in the bathroom, in all the cupboards.
No Wilbur. Then she looked in the computer room . . .

'OH NO!!!' cried Winnie.
'Wilbur, where are you? And where's the computer?'

She reached into the cupboard for her book of spells. She put her hand in her pocket for her magic wand.

Then she remembered.

She ran to the window. The dustman was tipping her rubbish into his truck.

'Stop!' shouted Winnie. 'STOP!' But it was too late. The dustman couldn't hear her. He jumped into his truck and drove away.

'What shall I do?' cried Winnie.

Then another truck came through the gate.
'My new wand!' said Winnie.
'It's arrived! Thank goodness!'

She grabbed the new wand, waved it once, and shouted,

ABRACA

The book of spells flew out of the rubbish truck, up into the air . . .

DABRA!

. . . and dropped into her arms.

Winnie rushed inside, and looked up the spell to make things come back.
Then she shut her eyes, waved her wand four times, and shouted,

ABRACADABRA!

The computer and Wilbur came back.
'Oh, Wilbur!' said Winnie. 'You're bright blue!
Whatever happened?
Never mind, I'll change you back to black again.'

She went to the computer
and clicked the mouse.
Wilbur was a black cat again.

'Good,' said Winnie.
'It still works. But I think I'll keep my
book of spells and my magic wand.
I might need them one day.'

Winnie
at the Seaside

It was a very hot summer.
Winnie the Witch felt hot and tired.
Wilbur, her cat, felt hot and tired, too.
'I want a swim, Wilbur,' Winnie said.
'Let's go to the seaside.'

Winnie found her beach towel, her
beach bag and her beach umbrella.

She jumped onto her broomstick,
Wilbur jumped onto her shoulder,
and they were off.

They flew over hot towns,
hot roads, hot cars,
and then they came to the sea.

There were lots of people on the beach,
but Winnie found a place for her towel.

She put up her beach umbrella
and got ready for her swim.

'Look after my bag and my broomstick, Wilbur,' Winnie said.
She ran into the water.

It was lovely in the sea.
Winnie splashed through the water,
and skipped over the little waves.
She was having a lovely time.

Wilbur sat and watched her.
He couldn't swim. He didn't like water.
He hated getting wet.

Winnie dived into the water. It was such fun!

But the water started to creep up the sand,
up to Winnie's towel.

Wilbur jumped onto
Winnie's beach umbrella.
'Meeow,' he cried.

Then the sea picked Winnie up, turned her
over three times, and dumped her on the sand.

The water washed over Winnie's towel,
and came half way up Winnie's beach bag.

'Meeeooooww,' cried Wilbur.
He didn't want to get wet.

'Oh dear,' said Winnie. She shook
some seaweed out of her hair.

'Don't worry, Wilbur.
   We'll just move further up the beach.'

She picked up her beach bag and her towel.
'My broomstick!' cried Winnie. 'Where's my broomstick?'

She looked everywhere.

No broomstick.

Then she looked out to sea.
There was her broomstick, floating away.

'Stop!' Winnie shouted.
But her broomstick didn't stop.

'How will we get home, Wilbur?' cried Winnie.
Then she had an idea.
She grabbed her beach bag, took out her
magic wand, waved it five times, and shouted,

ABRACADABRA!

The broomstick stopped.

Then it started to come back.

But a surfer was in the way.

WHOOSH

went the broomstick,
high up in the air,
and it landed on a whale.

The whale didn't want a broomstick on its back.

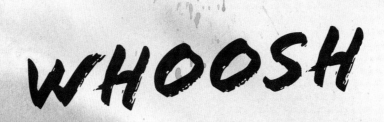

WHOOSH

went the broomstick, high up in the air,
in a great spout of water.

SPLASH!

Winnie's broomstick had come back.
Winnie was pleased.

The other people on the beach
were not pleased at all.

They were very WET.

Wilbur was not pleased either.
He was very wet, very sandy,
and rather squashed.

'Oh dear,' Winnie said. 'We'd better go home, Wilbur.'
She packed everything up.

Then Winnie and Wilbur zoomed up into the sky.

They were soon home again.
It was still hot in Winnie's garden.
Winnie still felt hot and tired.

Then she had a wonderful idea.

She took her magic wand out of her beach bag,
shut her eyes, turned around three times,
and shouted,

ABRACADABRA!

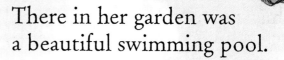

There in her garden was
a beautiful swimming pool.

Winnie dived in.

She swam up and down, and
then she floated on her back.

'This is lovely, Wilbur,' she said.
'It's much nicer than the seaside.'

Anything is nicer than the seaside, thought Wilbur.